Big Al's Christmas Wedding

By Patsy Stanley

ISBN 978-1-7328552-0-5

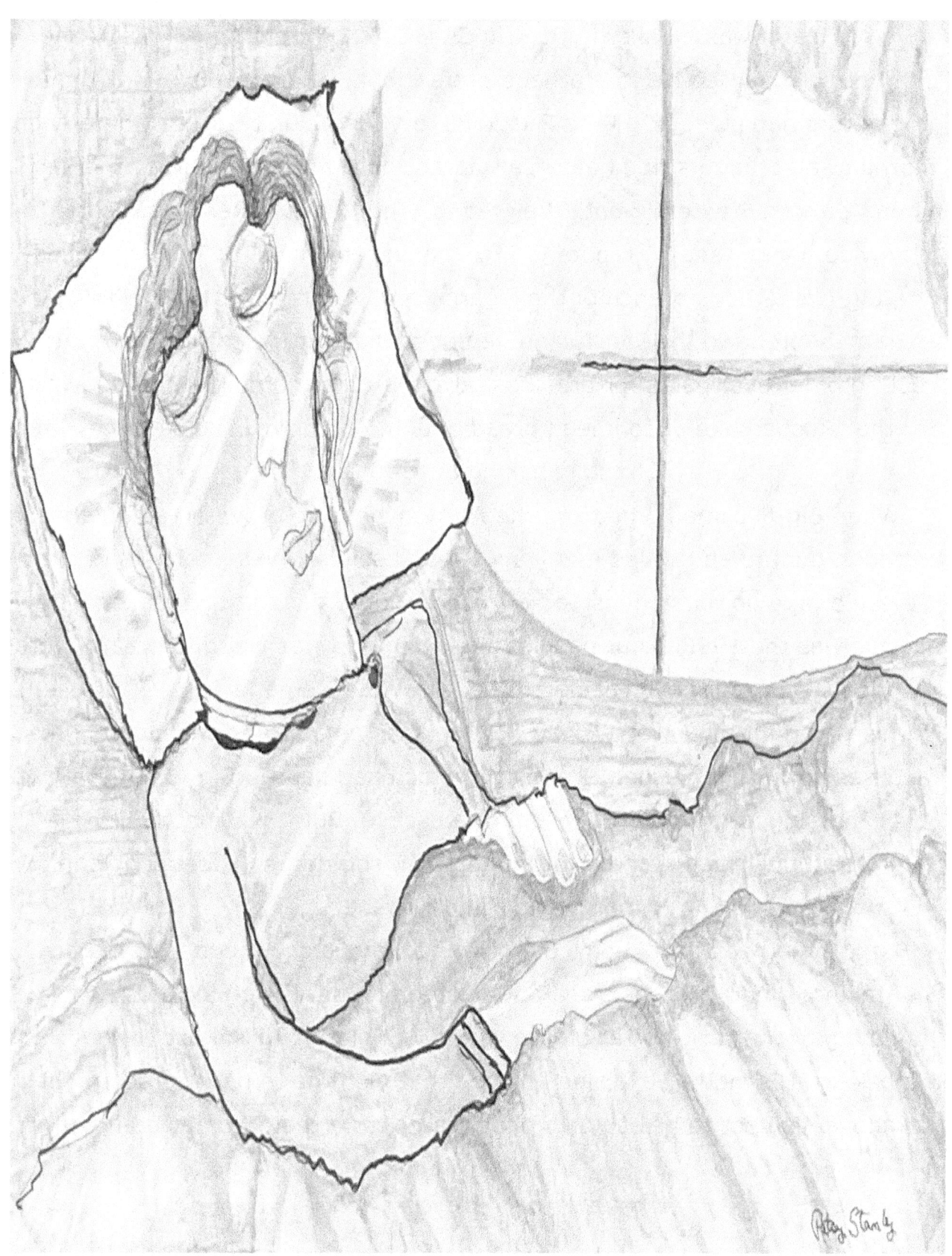

Big Al Figarin was a baker in the Big City, U.S.A, where he earnestly and thoroughly learned his forefather's professional baking skills. His tireless progenitors had pioneered "The Rustic Bakery" on Squint Street, where each morning, an orange striped alley cat glared through the window of the back room, purring insistently until they fed it. The Rustic Bakery maintained a city wide, long-standing reputation for making the finest of Tuscan breads.

Big Al's father's branch of the Figarin family were pious and reliable, extremely prone to the inertia and heftiness that long term sighing and the eating of leftover pasta for breakfast at two in the morning before leaving for the "Rustic Bakery" to knead bread dough, can bring. You see, they had to start baking at 4:40 am.

When Big Al came home from the Army, where he drove an ambulance through gunfire and saved many a wounded soldier, he sometimes wished he could take up nursing instead of a becoming a generational baker. After all, this was the 1950's, but people might think he was weird for yearning to work at what so many considered just a service woman's job. Of course, this was right after women had flown planes as backups and worked in factories during the Second Great War, which had caused Big Al to dream of nursing, and to think it might be possible. But it was not to be. Freedoms brought about for any reason, sometimes affect people in unsuspected ways.

Big Al's mother understood. Big Al was always a shy, gentle, caring boy, taking in hurt pigeons, repairing busted bicycles for crying kids and humming to the cat who sat on the windowsill glaring in the back window of the bakery. His mother explained to him that his urge to be a nurse and help someone else not to be sad or broken, came from the Stoomer branch, her side of the family.

1

She told her son he must never just sit about and become gravely damp over his yearning to be a nurse, or at a young age he could succumb to the horrible death of Faffle-dampening, a form of chronic inertia which had fatally afflicted many of her Stoomer relatives back in the Old Country. She told him that he must forestall and waylay the beginning of the dreaded disease of Faffling; that safety from the steady creep of Faffle-dampening caused by his yearnings, lay in his being content to knead bread, stir up frothy jams, and not question life too much.

Life was what it was, and it could be worse.

She told him this while putting on her apron and pinning up her hair before she began tossing fresh pasta and stirring tomato sauce. Big Al Figarin believed his mother, and in his younger days he tended to follow her advice. Big Al's full name was Albert Bertrand Figarin. During his school years the other students nicknamed him "Figgy" or "Bert", and tended to form impromptu choirs that sang operatic, foolish, schoolish versions of "Figaro" whenever he was around. He ignored them. He personally preferred Bertrand, but he was called "Big Al" by everyone except his mother, who always called him Albert, and, he suspected, always would. "Oh well" he said to himself, accepting life as it was, and not trying to change it too much to suit himself, as his mother had advised.

Big Al believed in God and in being well shod. Big Al became a big man with large feet precisely the proper size for someone nicknamed "Big Al". He wore the best of shoes because after all, he stood on his feet all day long in the bakery. His size shoes were hard to find, so he had his shoes made by Stan the Shoe Man, whose tiny shoe shop down on 157th Street held many mysterious leathers that Stan said came straight from the Australian Outback.

When people first saw his size and his large, well shod feet, they laughed and murmured to each other that Big AL owned a "good understanding". He hoped their words meant he was thoroughly grounded and predictably solid, something he yearned to be in order to avoid the dreaded Faffling from his mother's side of his family. He hoped their words were prophetic and true, but in fact, he wasn't very sure of much of anything.

Big Al was helpful to his mother and a good listener to his father, mostly because of being primitively bashful and myopically shy. He grew up to become an almost mute, restless man with eyes that searched everywhere, but lit nowhere. He didn't know what he was looking for, but he hoped fervently and bashfully to find it someday.

The family bakery was located two blocks west of the Golden Music Record Shop, a mom and pop establishment run by an old white-haired couple. Across the street from the record shop was a city park. Big Al sometimes went to the park and fed the pigeons while his predictable life went on. Like a large, smooth, polished stone, he moved through life with the usual expectations of family, friends, and strangers, simple expectations usually concerning bagels, small talk, and sometimes, frothy beer.

But there was more to Big Al than met the eye. Little did anyone in Big Al's donut frying, bagel tossing life suspect that he was a secret member of the Top Hat Club, a small, secretive band of reluctant, shy men who wore different hats fraught with meaning for the three days of the full moon each month. Their club was neither a first come first-serve club, nor a one-size-fits-all club, as would be people who owned hats, but were fraught with reasons to never, ever wear them.

The Top Hat Club met in secret once a week at an old movie theater and watched black and white movies of Fred and Ginger dancing.

3

This activity kept their damp, hopeful spirits up, their feet limber, and the threat of Faffling far away from Big Al.

When the full moon rose each month, as it always did, solid, golden or silver, each member of the small, secret band of reclusive, anxious, modest men donned that month's hat and voila! Instantly they changed into eager, outgoing, bold, brave heroes with a yen for acceptance in the right circles, in higher social echelons, and at the newspaper offices. During their three night heroic endeavors, they were gifted with a capacity for much verbiage, both loud and looming, concerning events that normally left them speechless.

The newly donned Top Hat heroes sprang into action at midnight on the three nights of the full moon each month. With hats atop, full moon shining above, their ardent, beating sternums filled with heart thumping romantic notions and brave, shining chivalry, they spread across the Big City in search of missions until 3:17am.

The Top Hat wearing, moon filled heroes helped late-night wanderers cross dark streets, supplied soup and Tuscan bagels to the hungry, set up pup tents in alleys for the homeless, some of whom had real pups, gave advice about the use of parking meters, and patiently explained directions to the city's lost or frightened late night tourists. They did as many good deeds as they could find to do, whether wanted or not, before retiring to their secret lair after 3 hours and 17 minutes of heroic work. They placed their Top Hats in neat rows, and returned to their homes like they'd been in bed snoring all night.

Unknown to Big Al Figarin, secret full moon superhero, Veretta Susan Beretta or "Vetta" as she was known to her pals, lived uptown in the Big City. In fact, she lived two blocks east of the Golden Music Record Shop, and she was a member of a secret hat club, too.

Over lonely, painful years, both Big Al and Vettas empty heart's had become barren, desert wastelands. With hearts as big as any full moon, theirs were pure, empty, huge golden hearts, just waiting for love to fill them. Both Big Al and Vetta visited the Golden Music Record Shop and listened to golden oldies and dreamed romantic dreams while their strong, lonely, misunderstood hearts, filled with unrequited love, beat steadily with valor, sincerity, Big Band and Doo Wop syncopations. Propinquity being what it is, Big Al and Vetta should have met in their youth while their hearts were still young. But East is east, and West is west, so they didn't. But there was another reason, a secret reason they never met.

Vetta visited the record shop during the three nights of the full moon each month, while Big Al was out doing heroic deeds with his top Hat club members, deeds wanted or not.

Big Al visited the record shop before and after his Top Hat full moon secret hero missions were over each month. That's when Vetta was out on her own secret club missions.

And so it was that the Fates designed their lives so that each one visited the record shop each month, but never met. Who can guess what the Fates will do next, as they are a willful bunch with reasons of their own? Reasons they never like to disclose, or they might not remain mysterious. And they might have to comb their hair.

Back home, late at night, nestled in their beds in their high, lonely lairs in the Big City, Big Al and Vetta listened to the music of a magical, romantic, bygone era, whilst dreaming of dancing and romancing. They dreamed of black tuxedos and white ball gowns, of Fred and Ginger dancing, of movie kisses that filled the silver screen, of being held close under a full moon. And so they lived separate and apart from each other and all the other lonely hearts dreaming their lives away in the Big City.

5

Maybe there were lessons to be learned before they could meet. Maybe it wasn't their destiny to meet. Or maybe there were other reasons. Who knows? One could securely count upon the Fates and Karma to be quirky…

The years passed. Big Al baked. Vetta became a Breck School girl. She took flying lessons and graduated fourth in her class, then took more flying lessons. She bought a small two-seater airplane and flew high above the Big City in her tiny plane, a tiny silver glint of reflected light moving above the buildings, searching below for something she could not name.

High above the Big City, like a bird, she flew. She wanted to keep flying forever. She wanted to fly away to a tropical island where an azure sea washed and sloshed around her in a great circle, bringing freedom to her while she swam or lay in the sun, contented and tan. But sooner or later she had to land and go home again. Before she landed, she always buzzed her home and the park near the record shop.

On his days off from the bakery, Big Al sometimes heard the drone of a small plane high above him. Each time he looked up, he saw a tiny plane reflecting silver in the sunlight above the tall buildings surrounding him. The little plane's shiny silver surface reflected the sun into his eyes, flashing down a message to him, a message similar to Morse code, which was foreign to him. He tried, but he couldn't decipher the message. Each time he gave up and let the mysterious code go.

Time flew by. Vetta stored her plane and hid her secret club hats in a far back closet. She determinedly became a housewife to a dashing Army man who went off to another land to get himself killed so he could become a posthumous Hero. He tried very hard to reach that goal. After a while he succeeded, leaving Vetta a tiny life insurance policy, four children, and a shiny medal to remember him by.

6

Vetta wiped their children's tears away, hired a babysitter, and went to work at a travel agency. Day-by-day she helped others dreams of visiting golden beaches and faraway places come true.

Big Al married too, and set aside his own secret hat club activities. He surreptitiously locked his hats away in a secret, temperature-controlled, sealed rental closet that no one else knew about, including his new bride. So it was that Big Al's treasured hats remained parted from him, but never forgotten. After storing them away, he moved three streets north to Bleaker Street with his new wife, whose father and mother lived alone in a big apartment above the drugstore where his father-in-law was the owner and pharmacist.

Three children and many stomach seltzers later, amid much chaos and a steadily growing fear of Faffling, Big Al divorced his wife in self-defense. She was a cook who tended to stay suspiciously thin and angry in response to Big Al's gentleness, while the children played loudly and constantly eroded his nerves, until he could take no more of either.

His mother and father-in-law, crestfallen at their daughters' divorce, and the fact she and the three bratty children would have to continue to live with them, sued him for all he was worth, which happened to be a few bagels of the Tuscan variety. "At least I get to keep my shoes made of that mysterious Australian Outback leather," Big Al thought.

Big Al was assigned child support to pay, after which he fled to the small back room of his family's bakery, where the orange striped cat glared in the window and watched his life without judgment, only hunger, and purred, and he hummed back to it, and fed it, with a sound pouring from his throat that sounded like the cooing of doves.

Big Al immediately breathed a sigh of relief into the healing silence of his

new dwelling. Though he felt he was a bad man for leaving, he knew he would have died if he stayed with his angry wife and uncaring, loud, sullen children. Better an absent father paying child support than one dead from rusted nerves and a few other rusty parts, he reasoned. He did not want to be dead. Or rusted.

From far back in the old days there still sputtered a tiny spark in him searching for something. That small spark helped him leave a bad situation. He felt guilty, sad and old, but alive. And that was as much as could be done at that time.

Once in awhile, during a busy day at the bakery, he stepped out into the street and studied the patches of blue sky high above the tall buildings, his eyes searching for the little plane that once flashed messages he never understood down to him. But it wasn't there anymore.

The days sped by, and the now fat, purring orange striped cat produced three kittens that first October. She taught them to line up at the window and glare and meow until Big Al fed them. The wind still blew high above the tall buildings in the empty sky above the Big City. All was predictable.

But change was on its way. Rain was coming. Some knew about that odd kind of rain. They shuddered, closed their windows, drew their curtains and hid. Early one morning, while the people in the Big City slept, the wind shifted out of its predictable patterns. It began to whistle across the tops of the skyscrapers in the Big City. The mysterious, steady rain began to fall. The orange cat and the three kittens glaring through the backroom window of the bakery stopped meowing. They sniffed the rainy air thoroughly, then ran and hid under the back stoop steps.

Later that same night, after a rain filled day at the bakery, Big Al strode purposefully through the mysterious mist towards the Golden Music Record Shop.

Mist and drizzle hid the moon from view above the Big City, but Big Al knew it was there. He'd rejoined the secret Top Hat Club after his life saving familial defection. Now it was time to visit the record shop again and take up another old, but good, true habit. The years had fled by since he last visited The Golden Music Record Shop. He yearned for it to still be the same.

Big Al was lonely, but he didn't want any more trouble. He settled for music, feeding four orange striped cats, and experimental baking to soothe his wounded soul. Instead of looking for a new relationship, which he found immensely terrifying, he invented the Sousa roll, a rustic, solid roll jammed full of hearty, loud notes of spicy beef, which sold like hot cakes at the bakery. In fact, the Sousa roll outsold the bakery's traditional hot cakes by 428%. At the time he was walking in the rain, he was just done being involved in sorting out the pros and cons of a Beethoven biscuit; the thorny dilemma there was achieving just the right amount of leavening to make it rise above the other rolls. Texture was the problem. The texture was too predictable, too morose, quite like Beethoven himself at times.

"It was probably good," Big Al mused, "that he was just a poor baker with three children to pay for, and not much to offer in the way of desirability to another woman."

He sighed sadly. For once, baking couldn't cheer him up, he needed new music tonight. Anything to lift him out of his slough of despond. If he remained in that slough much longer, it could bring on a serious case of the dreaded Faffling. He knew that the steady rain falling around him promoted the evil Faffling, and in fear of what might happen to him in his sad state, Big Al rushed towards the music shop, instinctively aware that something was ending for him. He was in grave danger of becoming a petrified Faffler!

Desperately, he imagined the notes of a fine, 78 rpm blues record pouring from his antique Victrola, perfectly matching his melancholy mood, picking up his sadness and tossing it away. He imagined the strains of mellow sounds sweeping across the backwash of misery he constantly carried, soothing it into oblivion, completely driving away the ever present threat of Faffling.

Soon he saw the familiar, fuzzy glow of neon through the rain, announcing that The Golden Music Record Shop was still in business. He heaved a great sigh, this time of relief, and hurried forward. As he drew close to the door, out of nowhere, a sudden gust of rain laden wind shoved him forward, causing him to run smack into someone, knocking them down.

Big AL leaned over the fallen individual. A faint scent of perfume wafted up to him. He sniffed. Evening in Paris. He knew it well. It was the same scent, except for the added scents of pastas and various sauces, his mother, grandmother, and all his many aunts wore. He sniffed again and knelt on the sidewalk besides the fallen person. Through the rain he detected the glistening outline of a small woman's thin form. She lay perfectly still, staring up at him with huge, silver eyes.

Big Al, dumbstruck and fear filled around women since his former unlucky marriage, couldn't speak. Instead, he did what he surmised to be the next best thing, which is what men have always done since the beginning. He scooped up the woman in his arms, and rushed through the front door of The Golden Music Record Shop.

The two faces of the white haired owner's turned to him in astonishment.

"Oh!" they said as he carried her in. "What happened?"

"I ran her down right outside the door," Big Al confessed in a shamed voice.

He followed the old couple past the Perry Como albums into a dimly lit, tiny back room.

A sofa crammed against the wall took up most of the tiny room. It was covered with a green chenille spread. Clumsy with remorse, Big Al gently laid his victim down on the sofa and stood up. He shook his head to clear it. It seemed to him like the talkative, lolling, blabby wind and the mysterious, clinging rain had somehow joined forces, and followed him into the tiny back room, for he was having a hard time seeing his victim.

He sensed the small thinness of her and knew that she was fastidious. Such truths were easy to form; they ran deep and stayed stalwart. He knew these things were true about the small, thin woman, for she smelled like maple syrup in the spring time, like the sap trees smelled when he once visited his uncle's farm as a boy. The wafting, sweet, spring laden scent with an undertone of winter, always transported Big Al momentarily, yet he knew where he currently was, but maybe not why.

He ran his hands across his face and sighed. A lot of time had passed since his boyhood, his uncle's farm, and now. Heaps of hope amid many smells, mainly of bagels and marinara sauces, had drained away, quickly, like hot soapy water pouring down a drain, or slowly, like a ball of foaming yeast that emitted bubbles, but couldn't rise anymore.

He held his large, meaty hands up and examined them. He assessed them as hard working, capable hands with clean nails. He looked down past his ample girth at his large, boot shod feet, and clasped his hands nervously for a moment. "People say I have a good understanding, then they laugh at me." He thought to himself. "But I don't know anything. I don't know the first thing about anything except bagels."

Suddenly he found himself kneeling beside the sofa, stroking the hair back from the small woman's white, frightened face. She stared up at him while the involuntary cooing sound, like that of a dove, rose and poured forth

11

from deep in his throat his throat like it did with the orange striped cats when he petted them, except he allowed it with them, but only when no one else was around.

Aghast and embarrassed at the unexpected sound that had poured spontaneously from him, he pressed his lips tightly together. But he was not to be stopped. He gingerly pressed the woman's arms and legs to see if they were injured. After he rotated her ankles, flexed her hands, and counted her fingers and toes, he stood up.

He eyed her. She lay there in a white cotton frock frothed with a bunch of layers of lace. The dress had seen better days. Big Al could not have surmised or known the dress was her mother's wedding dress. The woman's pale, silver-eyed face was framed with a wild, disorderly mass of honey colored hair generously laced with streaks of white. She owned a sharp, pointy, stubborn-looking chin and a tough looking, tiny rosebud mouth tucked under a long nose. In short, determination was threaded through her essence. Her eyebrows rose like the wings of crows above her prominent, thick lidded eyes.

Then her hat came into focus. Perched askew on her head as if it were ready to spin off into the air at any moment, sat a tiny black Fascinator hat of black velvet with pert, semi-stiff black netting hovering just above her left eye. Big Al was beguiled. He sucked in his breath. She was beautiful, the most beautiful woman he'd ever seen, except Greta Garbo, or his mother, of course…or maybe Janie Rohr in sixth grade.

He sucked in his breath at the realization, carefully removed his top hat, then backed out of the tiny room. He turned and rushed outside. The pushy, sweeping wind and the blabby, mysterious rain were gone. Their jobs of nudging some, and sometimes none, towards their new fates, were done. Big Al stared up at the large, waning moon glowing boldly in the clear, dark

sky, bathing it in generous, magnanimous light.

He ruminated, scuffling his feet, remembering his grandfathers electrifying words as different doctors worked him over while Big Al waited. "Run!" He said, staring up at the moon. Yes, he knew many people scoffed at the idea of secret clubs filled with part time heroes who sought to accomplish good deeds during the full moon.

Big Al was glad he was a member of the secret Top Hat Club again. This month they practiced old fashioned chivalry and traditional ballroom dancing featuring the Foxtrot at 3:20 a.m. each night. Next month would be a different hat along with a different topical, or sometimes tropical dance in which the ability to glide, slide, and sway played an important role. Big Al was renowned in the club for his catlike grace while sliding.

Frozen where he stood, Big Al Figarin stared up at the moon as he recalled rumors of a secret women's Top Hat Club swayed by the waning pull of each month's moon into becoming heroines. It was said that they were strong, silly, romantic women who yearned for a knight in shining armor; that's what he'd heard, or so it was rumored.

Was she one of them? Surely he was mistaken. Surely it was only a legend. Still, it was rare to see a woman wearing a hat. And, the woman's tiny black Fascinator hat perfectly matched his black top hat.

As Big Al stood on the sidewalk, staring up at the moon, the woman stepped outside and stood close to him. Her lovely scent wafted up to his nostrils, bringing happy memories of tall stacks of pancakes laden with maple syrup, organic butter, and 3 large eggs with crisp bacon and 2 cups of hot, steaming coffee laden with a dash of cream, imbibed from 3:10 a.m. to 3:40 a.m. in a warm, busy kitchen before work began at 4:40 a.m.

He sniffed deeply and looked down at her. She looked up at him. They studied each other.

13

He thought she was too thin; he was a baker after all. She thought he smelled like bagels. She liked bagels. He had a safe and delicious smell. After a moment, he reached out his arm for her to take, then led her to the dinner restaurant down the street where Ralph the waiter played piano. He ordered for her as she didn't seem inclined to speak. His order would have been pancakes with maple syrup if it hadn't been a dinner restaurant. She partook of French onion soup in quick tiny sips and tore a soft bagel apart, taking tiny, bird-like bites while watching him with great, silver eyes. After she ate, she stood up and darted out the door, quick and quiet as any shadow. Big Al reached out his hand to stop her, but he had to stay behind and pay the bill. When he burst out the door, she was gone...

Big Al strolled casually into the record shop at exactly ten o'clock the following night. All day long, while he kneaded bread dough and agitated chocolate for blissful pies at the bakery, he thought of nothing but the silver eyed woman in the ragged wedding dress.

He took off his top hat and looked around. He wandered back and forth among the displays of fine old records as the hour grew later and later. Dessie and Lou, the white haired owners, watched him from their chairs behind the checkout counter until they finally dozed off, leaning against each other in their tall chairs, instead of ushering him out and locking the door behind him. The large, cat-faced clock on the wall behind the checkout counter loudly ticked away the minutes in the silent record store. Big Al stood planted in place, leaning against a record stand, remembering another time he had taken his grandfather to the doctor.

14

The cat faced clock made him a little nervous; he hoped it wasn't a wild cat clock, for it reminded him of his father's branch of the Figarin's, who all proudly owned wild cuckoo clocks that adorned the walls of their dining rooms, clocks that cuckooed exactly while the soup was being slurped, causing startled stains to arrive on time on table and laps, and just in general, cuckooing whenever they wanted to, which made for many shades of indigestion.

Vetta appeared just as midnight settled over the Big City. She wore the same frothy white garment and the little black Fascinator hat from the night before. She made no pretense of looking at the shop's many fine vinyl offerings from the Thirties, Forties and Fifties. No Perry, no Frank, no Les Brown, no Red Nichols or Tommy Dorsey. She walked straight up to Big Al, huge silver eyes staring up into his myopic, brown, yet hopeful eyes; she placed her hand daintily on his arm.

Big Al jerked a white handkerchief out of his pocket, hastily mopped his brow, then fumbled his pocket almost ragged trying to put his handkerchief away. After regaining composure, he offered her his arm and they strolled sedately out of the record shop.

He locked the door behind him to keep the napping old folks safe, then led the tiny woman to the restaurant where Ralph the waiter played piano again.

That night, she slurped long strands of spaghetti and valiantly chewed doughy and aromatic garlic bread. He took a chance with words.

"I like your hat," he said gravely.

She nodded, then pointed to the top hat he wore. She motioned out the window at the moon before she stood up and hurried out the door. He sucked in his breath. So she did know about Top Hat moons! A ridiculous thing to the uniformed, but important to those like him, who yearned to be a different kind of hero or heroine!

15

Vetta raced down the street. Her destination was home, and she was determined to reach the safety of her familiar nest as quickly as possible. She was a brave woman, but she was frightened to death of having another hero in her life. The last one had brought her many children, a slew of bills and great loneliness. As a result, she had taken a vow of silence when it came to another romance in her life. And Vetta always kept her vows.

Besides, there were the children to think of.

But as we know, those willful Fates will have their way. Late that night, Vetta dreamed of marrying Big Al on the stroke of midnight in a silver misted, moonlit church. In her dream, it was Christmas Eve. She wore her mother's wedding gown and carried silver misted roses. Her bridesmaids were snappily dressed and happy. She was happy. Her parents were not happy. Everyone has an opinion. Even in dreams.

Vetta woke up, jumped out of bed. She paced the floor. She had to work the next day, but this was important! After a long, doubt- ridden conversation with herself, she came up with the only possible answer. It was an answer that would involve a great deal of compromise and patience on both their parts. She would see in time, if her plan for their future worked out. After all, her children were still young and needed her. She could find no other solution. She just hoped Big Al would understand, and go along with her plan.

The next night, Vetta met Big AL at the record store. She kept her vow of silence. They dined again and then parted. In time, Big Al realized they were to learn about each other without words. He came to understand that Vetta needed to have it that way for reasons he did not know, but should accept. And he did. After a while, he realized the wordless plan Vetta made, was best for him, too, for he also had young children to raise.

16

So Big Al turned to tango and experiments with yeasty brews of bread dough once again to pass the time.

September's full moon arrived. Vetta met Big Al at the record store wearing a gray cloche hat. Her hat matched his Trilby. They stopped a distracted man from walking out in front of a car before they dined and danced the fox trot in the lamp lit park at the corner of 4th and Main, then discreetly parted.

Each month, for three glorious nights during the full moon, with unspoken consent and no words exchanged, they met at the record shop to stroll the aisles, their empty hearts filling to near bursting with un-heard music. Good deeds and good dinners followed, during which they stared at each other and memorized the contours and lines of each other's faces.

They each accepted their odd situation, though it was more than odd to some others who viewed it as a trial or a tribulation; including Ralph the waiter and white haired Dessie and Lou. Neither one of them was free to go any farther in their relationship anyway. Both had no spouses, but each had a brood of children who were only half-raised.

For five years, Big Al and Vetta met at the record shop once a month and celebrated the Top Hat moons.

In October, Big Al donned his Wallaby hat from Down Under, while Vetta wore an English riding hat. They delivered baskets of food to needy families, ate late night dinners, and danced the Argentine Tango under the El at 50th and 3rd Streets.

Wearing Mist hats in November, they delivered fresh fruit and cut flowers to a local home for the elderly, then did the Stroll down Central and 25th Streets before enjoying dinner at The Oyster Shack.

17

December's snow blanketed the Big City. Vetta donned her Fedora Hunting hat. Big Al wore his Deerstalker. They passed out blankets to the homeless, dined at the Steak Palace and danced short, quick Marimbas before quickly parting.

In January, Vetta wore a Mourning hat with the black veil pinned up. Big Al donned a Bowler. With a dignity befitting the dead, they served hot soup to the homeless in Pink's Alley, then somberly danced the Hesitation Waltz in the Ashbury cemetery on the corner of Bleak and Pine.

In February, Vetta donned a knit Beanie with side flaps to keep her ears warm while Big Al wore his Beaver Hat. They danced the East Coast swing outside the bus station downtown after handing out coffee, donuts, and sandwiches to the many weary travelers within.

March brought silliness and sack lunches on the Top Hat nights. Vetta wore a Mushroom hat. Big Al wore his Porkpie hat. They ran errands for a shut-in and shoveled snow and salted the sidewalk in front of an elderly man's home before they dined, then danced the Cha-Cha-Cha at the foot of the waterfall on Fountain St.

In April, Vetta wore a Veiled hat. Big Al wore a Homburg. It was perfect headgear for passing out food trays to the senior residents of the Valley View Shelter downtown. Their hats were perfect, as well, for dancing the Mambo on Loon St.

In May, Vetta's Garbo hat made her seem even more mysterious to Big Al. He wore his Derby and they dined at Mac's Burgers and danced the Macarena in front of the record store after helping a family move into a nearby apartment.

In June, she wore a dimpled leather Beanie. He wore his Aviator's cap. They cut a dashing picture as they assisted two ladies to their homes, dined,

18

and later waltzed in the middle of the Green Bridge, who everybody knows, almost touches the sky, causing dreams to come true.

In July they strolled through the zoo in Panama hats and dined at the Salty Buffet. They delivered stuffed animals to the children's shelter in Upper Big Town, then danced the Paso Doble around the Art Center Statues at Green and West St. before they parted.

In August, their routine began all over again. Vetta donned her tiny black Fascinator. Big Al donned his velvety black Top Hat. It was their first year anniversary. They ate salads while listening to Ralph play piano. Later they waltzed high atop the Green Bridge at midnight.

Well, as we all know, seasons pass and dance crazes end. Well, at least some. Each Top Hat Moon came and went with Big Al and Vetta earnestly yearning for the verbiage and tender touches from one another only true love can bring. But just like it has always been for the rest of us at one time or another, it was not yet time for their love to blossom into its fullness. They were able to wait steadfastly, for from their beginning, from the very moment they met each other, they were two people used to being in the predicament of having to live quiet, duty filled lives, lives filled with unrequited romance, lives barren and bereft of the love they both longed for.

Five years later, close to Christmas, both of their nests were at last empty. Their duties had been met. Big Al's hair was gray and white. Vetta's hair was silver, for their children had led them on many merry and otherwise-chases. Vetta began dreaming of the perfect Christmas wedding, of being married at midnight in a silver misted church wearing her mother's wedding dress,

refurbished, of course; of fragrant candles, red and green holly, mistletoe, and Christmas carols sung before the wedding march. She dreamed of a long, slow, well-earned walk down the aisle to meet Big Al at the altar and finally make him hers!

But it was not to be.

Big Al, who had been numbed to speechlessness with women, mainly his ex-wife and mother before meeting his lovely Top Hat moon lady; he who had gone five years without speaking to the true love of his life, became terrified of what would happen to them if he actually spoke to her.

They met in the record shop night after night while Vetta waited for him to speak. This was the fifties; after all, convention said it was the man's job to begin their first conversation. Break the ice. Open the door, as it were. But alas, although he put forth a mighty effort, Big Al remained speechless, his fear flying high as a kite in a strong wind over the Big City.

One cold winter night, the 1st of December it was, after a last futile attempt, he gave up. They had waited too long. The five years of silence and all that had gone before it, could not be overcome by Big Al. It was over. All had been in vain. He would never see Vetta again.

He left her standing in the record shop, alone, by the alphabetized albums of the greatest love songs ever recorded, featuring Mario Lanza, Bing, Louie and Ella, and dragged himself out the door, his wide shoulders slumped in despair, his large shoes tapping slowly along.

Vetta watched him go, her plans of a Christmas wedding crumbling into ruins. She counted the three weeks left until Christmas; three weeks and then the many terrible years of loneliness to follow. She pulled out her great-grandmother's tiny lace handkerchief from her purse, and began to sob into it. Then she felt a tap on her shoulder.

Vetta stared at the old white haired couple standing in front of her. The elderly gentleman held a bottle in his hands, and his wizened wife held a shot glass in her hands. "Don't cry! Drink this instead, Miss Susie Simple Slowdance Girl!" Dessie and Lou ordered sternly. "It's 1926 tax free, Prohibition scotch, Miss Nancy Not so Smart!"

They poured a drink, shoved it into her hand. Vetta gulped the scotch down in one wallop and wheezed until she got her breath again. They filled her shot glass again while chattering words of encouragement at her.

"Go get the Big Bagel Baking Lug, Miss Beanie Bird Blockhead!"

"Don't give up on that Noodle Headed Baker, Miss Foolish Flying Fanny! It's almost Christmas! Go after that Half Baked, Out to Lunch, Looney Tune Ham, that Page of Pounds, right now!"

Vetta emptied her shot glass again. Dessie and Lou refilled it and improvised, "Its stormy weather for Dim Dozey Cuckoo Birds like you two to get together! Giddy up, git' the hell outta' here, go after that Baffled, Luna Fat headed, dimly Lit Earl of Bacon, Miss Not Too Bright! It's got to be time to move on!" Dessie and Lou looked at each other in desperation.

Encouraged, with a flushed face full of hope and wonderment at their odd choices of words and songs, Vetta belted out, "As long as you love me so, let it snow, let it snow, let it snow."

She held the shot glass with both hands and emptied it while they sang, just covering all the bases they could, a bit of "Auld Lang Syne" and "Frosty, the Snowman".

A look of grim determination mixed with astonishment came over Vetta's face. She tossed the shot glass aside and staggered past them and out the door of the record store. Dessie and Lou cheered her on in frail voices. They had been forced to watch this never ending love story unfold at a snail's pace for the past long, oh so long!- five years. They'd patiently watched as it slowly and never endingly unfolded through snow and sleet and rain and hail. They'd patiently kept the vigil as Big Al and Vetta's romance crawled along through sunshine and sonic booms, amid the inevitably sad news that yet another golden oldie songbird had passed away. They knew all about time. They lost friends, celebrated anniversaries and birthdays, and adjusted their meds to juggle the complications of the erstwhile love played out in the back by the racks of golden oldies, including Perry Como. Well, it was now or never; they had listened to Perry Como long enough!

Besides having Como's Moon River and Dream Along With Me stuck in their heads like old bubblegum, Lou and Dessie had lost plenty of sleep because of the budding romance between the two silly sweethearts, both shy beyond reckoning, both shy beyond any version of reasonable sanity. More to the point, it just wasn't good for old folks like them to lose sleep at their ages.

Those kiddos weren't the only ones suffering!

They wanted it to end, to be finished, completed, concluded, so they could finally get their well-deserved naps and more rest. Babysitting a romance was not in their repertoires anymore. But they also wanted it to end with good results, so they would be invited to a wedding instead of yet another funeral. They were sick and tired of sorrow and buying sympathy cards by the baker's dozen. They needed a break!

They knew Big Al was a baker, and they suspected, a good one. They agreed that he was not a slacker, but he was definitely taking too long on this project, and the little bit of prohibition whiskey Vetta imbibed, just might help them out, give someone, anyone! - the needed boost, to get off the roost, one might say. Dessie and Lou grinned at each other in bleak hope.

22

Vetta staggered down the street in her mother's wedding frock. She pictured her mother. Her mother always knew better.

Big Al truly believed it was truly over, but in her drunken Christmas heart Vetta knew it wasn't. Along with the booze and the new hope planted in her heart by the insistent, shot glass filling, doo wop carol or whatever-singing old couple, Vetta made a new, daring, bold plan; she could never give up dreaming of her groom!...

Big Al was afraid to go back to the record shop the next night. Instead, he spent his time in the park across the street from it, staring at the record shop and sighing wistfully. It was the same park where he once rescued cats from trees, and carried home pigeons with broken wings to fix when he was a boy.

But he couldn't fix this. It was over. He sighed constantly, a sure sign of the beginning of the dreaded Stoomer Faffling disease, while somberly walking the snow plowed paths under the Christmas lights in the park. A light snow began falling, but Big Al never noticed the beauty around him. He was doomed. Yes, the dreaded Faffling was starting to take over.

Big Al's thoughts grew darker as he plodded along in the cold. His thoughts became larger, more terrible, more horrible, and downright mystifying.

"Yes," he thought. "It won't be long now before I am Faffled to death."

How would he end his final days? He would never find love again. There was nobody like Vetta. The speechless, lovely, mute woman who dressed so funny and frothy, the woman who taught him the power of silence and waiting and enduring with only a skimpy ounce of requited love in return, was lost to him forever because of his lack of words.

"Yes," he thought sadly. "I may as well let the Faffling get me."...

The next night at exactly 11:30 p.m., not a moment later, Vetta, wearing her cloche hat, flew over the tree tops in the park in her two-seater plane.

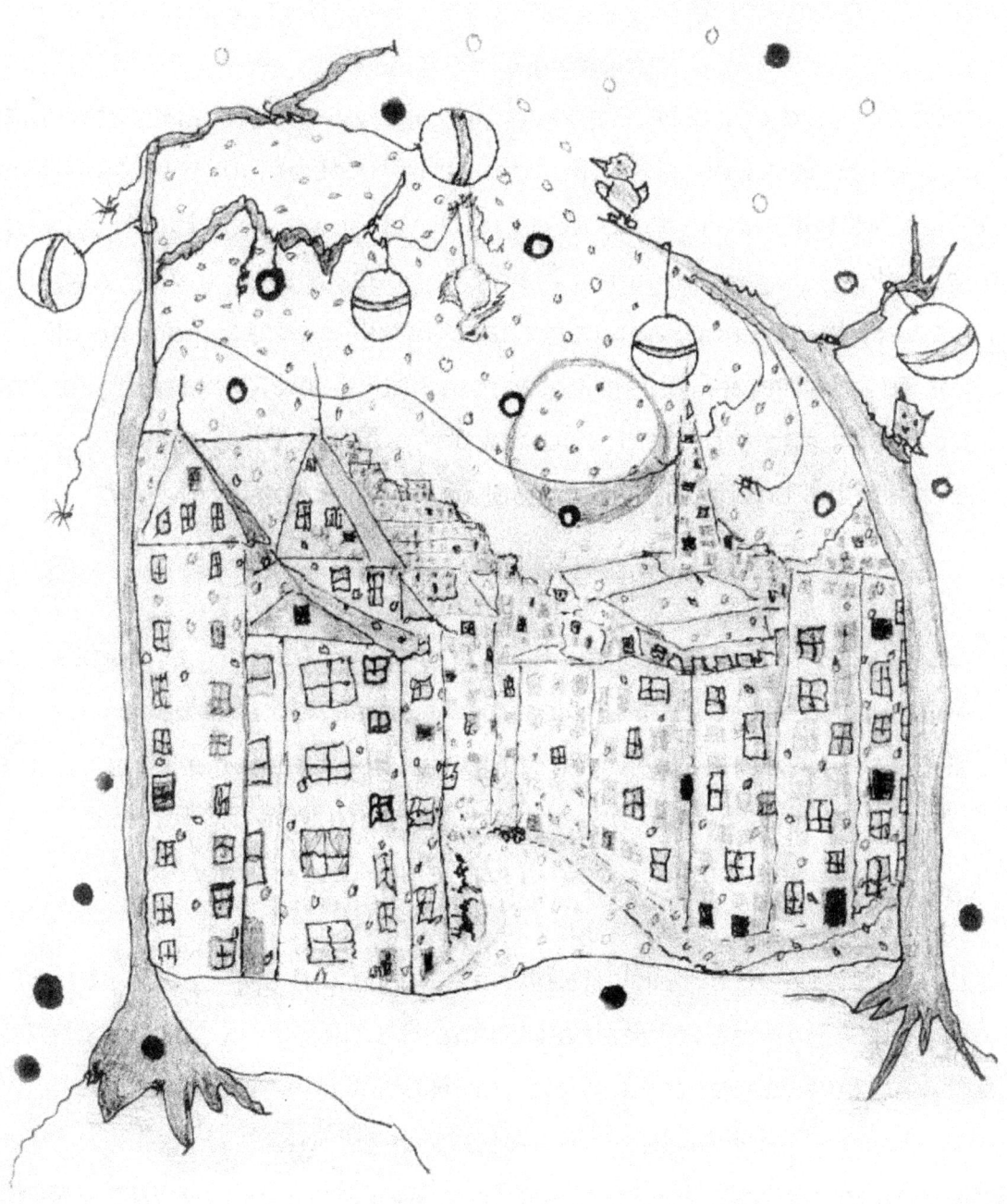

Maybe it was the right hat, maybe not. Frankly, she didn't give a damn. Bottom lines were bottom lines, and she had written one, literally, and it was time to deliver it.

The full moon beamed down on Big Al as Vetta buzzed him in her little plane, dropping a Christmas package on the ground in front of him. It was wrapped in shiny green foil with a big red bow on it. Vetta flew away. Big Al picked up the festive package and opened it. Inside the package lay a very large ring for his very large hand, a baker's hand familiar with yeast and all varieties of Tuscan bagels, plus a note from his fair maiden asking for that same large hand in marriage. He stared down at the tiny, white, hopeful note fluttering in his big hand. A proposal as it were. She'd given him a way past his shy speechlessness and fears.

Sometimes somebody else has to step in to get the job done, and Vetta was one to step up to the plate, so to speak. A plate not filled with bagels yet, but oh well. Big Al sighed again, this time in admiration. What a woman! This was the way out of his dilemma! Big Al seized the paper tightly, and in that instant, gave up being endangered by Faffle stalking forever. The Stoomer branch of his family would have to strike elsewhere to continue their legacy of Faffling!

Vetta buzzed him again in her little plane. He looked up, waved at her and shouted, "Yes!" Then he laughed and danced a tiny, suave jig before he hurried away to tend to his Top Hat full moon duties.

There was going to be a wedding!...

Big Al's widowed grandfather frankly didn't give a damn. He was safely on the other side of the family from those silly Stoomer Faffling folks. Their soppy, wet genetics weren't going to get him down! He was a survivor of many things, including World War One for one, and a few too many weddings of his own, for another.

24

Both bore striking similarities, one to the other, in his view. He studiously avoided all weddings like the plague ever since his last one. Bad is bad and worse is sometimes worse.

Then he saw a picture of Vetta's widowed grandmother, and quickly changed his mind. She was undeniably gorgeous, bountifully laden with veritable bossy knowledge, a fine full figure borne upon small feet that turned out, proud with hallowed wrinkles of experiences of all kinds, and loaded with busty, extra-cranky mileage; just like him, except for the bust and small feet. He decided then and there that he better get himself spruced up for the wedding, just in case.

First he went to the chiropractor, who loosened him up. Then he went to the doctor for heart pills, just in case. When the doctor was finished with him, he went shopping for a new suit and new long john underwear. After all, a man has to stay warm and keep his pulse up, or he could become frigid and die! And this WAS winter!

At last he looked in the mirror, slicked back his scant hair, and deemed himself ready for Big Al and Vetta's wedding. More than a marriage might be in the offing. Maybe a little side of romance, too? Who knew? His chances were good, for wasn't he a handsome Romeo back in the day, melting women's hearts and making them yearn for him while Frank and Perry sang love songs in the background?...

Twas' midnight on Christmas Eve. The church, inside and out, was enveloped in a magical silvery mist pouring down from the full moon above. All of the secret Top Hat club members, both his and hers, were in attendance, all dressed in the proper full moon attire.

Both the children and relatives who were, and weren't angry with Big Al

and/or Vetta attended their wedding. After all, nobody's perfect!

The Wedding March began, played by Ralph the waiter.

Truly, actions speak louder than words. Big Al and Vetta had kept their faith in each other. After five years of Top Hat moons and steadfast silences filled with searching looks and appraisals of each other, they knew they should always be together. They had more than paid their dues. A few others attending their wedding also agreed that they too, had paid quite a few dues themselves on the couple's behalf. Topping the list were Lou and Dessie, the white haired couple from the record shop, Ralph, the piano playing waiter from the restaurant they frequented just down the street from the record shop, and Benny the tailor, for beginners. Digressions are sometimes good for building suspense, but in some cases, like this one, as it has always been rumored, the less said, the better.

Their first spoken words to each other were, "I do."

A spaghetti supper was held in the basement of the church with Lou and Dessie happily presiding over the wedding cake, the scotch, and all the baked goods.

Vetta threw the bouquet after the dancing started. Her grandmother caught it and smiled meaningfully at Big Al's grandfather, who grinned and clicked his false teeth as he quickly sidestepped towards the closest exit.

Big Al and Vetta grabbed each other's hands and ran out to the church parking lot. Everyone followed them and cheered them on as they climbed into Vetta's little silver misted plane that held just room enough for two. Their destination was unknown, but they knew touchdown included the soothing, comforting verbiage and sweet, shy embraces both had forsaken for the sake of their beloved others for so long...

r the rest of the story, and how many Christmases they would share together, only time will tell. And so, bathed with Top hat Moonlight, with the Fates chuckling smugly, Big Al and Vetta flew off into their future beneath the twinkling Christmas stars!

Merry Christmas!

The End

More of Patsy Stanley's Christmas books!

Christmas Stories From the Crones Castle

The Baker's Christmas Wedding

Minnow Minnowfin's Christmas Tune-up- (A toy car story)

Grimy Toes McGrumpy

George Yodelsteen and Yodel Peak Mountain

The Christmas Standoff at Moose Hollow

Patsy Stanley Book Series

The Desert Store Series- 7 books-
1.Cowboy Johnson's Desert Oasis
2.The Red Cactus Desert
3.The Three Cactus Limbo
4.Susan Sugar Diamond
5.The Red Cactus orphanage
6.Manfred's Folly
7. The Points of Light

The Desert Store Series (7-Book Collection)
By Patsy Stanley — Blue WaterCress Ink: Books with Soul and Spark

In the wide, quiet stretch of the New Mexico desert, an old white church has been turned into a small store—simple, weathered, and sitting on land that holds something unseen. People find it when they need it most. They come and go—good people, each carrying their stories. Not flashy. Not loud. But real. The kind of goodness that sees deeper, feels stronger, and refuses to turn away from what matters. They build lives. They leave. They return. And somehow... they are always drawn back to the store. At the center are Cowboy Johnson and William the Dude, along with a growing circle of wounded healers, artists, fighters, mothers, wanderers, and misfits. Each one is changed by the store—and by each other. What begins as a place of refuge becomes something more. A gathering point. A testing ground. A call. Because beyond the ordinary world, something is shifting. A quiet war is forming—Good against a darker, older, Evil that is determined to take hold. These men and women, misfits with nothing but their quirks, insight, courage, and hard-earned wisdom, will stand together. No guns. No ammunition. Only what they carry within them. And what they have learned from nature.

Across seven books, their lives intertwine—through love, loss, truth, and transformation—until each must decide who they are, what they stand for, and how far they're willing to go for the light. Because the Desert Store was never just a place. It was a beginning.

Metaphysical Series- 6 books
1. The Spiritual Nature of Atomic Structure.
2. The Elements
3. Chakras, Meridians, and the Color Energies
4. Shield Energies
5. The Mental body
6. Sound Energies

The Energy Within- My Metaphysical Series

Patsy Stanley — Blue WaterCress Ink: Books with Soul and Spark

Why I Wrote These Books

by Patsy Stanley

I didn't set out to write a series about energy. When I was young, I searched. I studied the Vedas. I listened to teachers from many paths— some traditional, some not. I learned from Native American teachings, from spiritual seekers, from those who had walked long roads before me. I wasn't looking for one answer. I was trying to understand what was underneath all of them. Then, during an initiation, I was given an assignment I didn't expect. I was told to write about atomic structure. Not as a scientist—but as someone who had to understand how energy actually works. It didn't make sense at the time. But I accepted it. What followed was not a quick project. It became a twenty-year journey. I gathered material, studied, questioned, and tested what I was learning. I watched how energy moved through people, through choices, through consequences. I looked for patterns—real ones, not imagined ones. Over time, something became clear: Spiritual teachings speak in symbols. Science speaks in structure. But they are describing the same thing. I didn't want to write something vague or mystical just for the sake of it. I wanted it to be accurate. So I hired an ex-nuclear physicist to review the material—to make sure that what I was saying held up, not just spiritually, but scientifically. These books are the result. They are not meant to tell you what to believe. They are meant to show you how energy-life- work. Because once you begin to understand energy—how it moves, how it forms, how it affects your life—you start to see your choices differently. You start to see yourself differently. And maybe, like I did, you begin to realize...There is nothing random about any of this.

The Little Drought Stories-3 books

1. The Great and Most Horrible Little Drought
2. The Most Grumpy Little Drought
3. Whisperdust, the Wandering Drought

The Little Drought Stories

By Patsy Stanley — Blue WaterCress Ink: Books with Soul and Spark

Not all droughts are mean. Some are just... mistaken. In these whimsical, heart-tugging tales, the droughts that wander into the land aren't always villains—they're often small, confused, and a little too curious for their own good. What begins as trouble—dry rivers, wilting fields, grumbling creatures—turns out to be something else entirely. An innocent mistake. A lesson waiting to be learned. A bit of mischief that nature knows how to set right. With the help of unexpected heroes, talking winds, clever creatures, and the quiet wisdom of the natural world, each drought is met not with force—but with understanding, patience, and just the right nudge in the right direction. These stories are funny, gentle, and full of heart—reminding readers that even the biggest problems can come from the smallest misunderstandings......and that nature, in its own way, always knows how to heal what's gone a little wrong. *For readers ages 6 to 106—because even grown-ups can forget how simple some truths can be.*

Native American-2 books

1.Red leaf

2.The Green Mountain Shaman

Red Leaf and The Green Mountain Shaman

Two Short Stories by Patsy Stanley — Blue WaterCress Ink: Books with Soul and Spark

These stories were not imagined. They were lived. For thirteen years, I returned to the Rosebud Reservation in South Dakota—spending weeks learning, observing, and participating in sacred ways of life. Through Sun Dance, sweat lodge and vision quest and the everyday rhythms of the people, I was allowed to stand near traditions that are rarely explained and never taken lightly. These short stories are not teachings claimed or lessons owned. They are reflections—of moments, of people, of presence. Through the voices of Red Leaf and the Green Mountain Shaman, and others who have walked those paths, the reader is invited into a world where spirit is not separate from life. These two short stories are shared with deep respect. They do not represent or attempt to explain the full depth of Lakota or Native American spiritual traditions. They are personal reflections of time spent in proximity to these practices and people, and are offered in humility, not authority.

The Toy Car Series-
1.Minnow Minnowfin and the Missing Hood Ornament
2.Minnow Minnowfins Christmas Tune-up
3.Minnow Minnowfin's Snowstorm Rescue

The Toy Car Stories Series

By Patsy Stanley — Blue WaterCress Ink: Books with Soul and Spark

  The toy car stories were born in small, beautiful moments of childhood. Inspired by the days spent watching her son—and later her grandson—lost in the world of their toy cars, Patsy Stanley brings those memories to life in this charming and heartfelt series. In garages, on living room floors, and along imaginary roads that stretch far beyond the edge of a rug, toy cars come alive after hours. They form friendships, go on daring rescues, solve mysteries, and sometimes get into just a little bit of trouble. Each story captures the spirit of boyhood play—where a simple car becomes a hero, a journey, a whole world. Filled with adventure, humor, and heart, these tales celebrate imagination, loyalty, and the quiet magic of growing up. Because long after the toys are put away...the memories keep rolling. *For readers ages 6 to 106—and for anyone who remembers the sound of little wheels on the floor.*

Christmas Books

1. Christmas Stories from the Crones Castle
2. Big AL's Christmas Wedding
3. A Frost and Tumble Peak Christmas
4. The Bakers Christmas Wedding
5. George Yodelsteen and Yodel Peak Mountain
6. Grimy Toes McGrumpy
7. The Christmas Standoff at Moose Hollow

The Christmas Stories Collection

By Patsy Stanley — Blue WaterCress Ink: Books with Soul and Spark
There's something about Christmas that invites a little extra magic... and a lot of laughter. In this delightful collection of holiday stories, Patsy Stanley blends warmth, humor, and imagination into tales filled with mischievous elves, unexpected surprises, and the comforting smell of cookies fresh from the oven. These are not quiet, polished Christmas stories. They are lively. A little crooked. Full of heart—and just enough mischief to keep things

interesting. From grumpy mountains to stubborn characters, from odd happenings to joyful turnarounds, each story carries the spirit of Christmas in its own unique way—reminding us that wonder doesn't have to be perfect to be real. Written from a genuine love of the season, these stories celebrate the small moments, the laughter, and the magic that shows up when we least expect it. Because at Christmas…anything can happen—especially when imagination is invited in. *Perfect for readers ages 6 to 106—and for anyone who believes a good story and a warm cookie can fix just about anything.*

Novels- Love in later life

1.Addition Jones

2. Avalon Blue's Quest

3. The Color Blue of the Hermit's Robe

4. Big Otis, Miss May, and the OK Corral Bar-b-q.

Late-Life Love Stories

By Patsy Stanley — Blue WaterCress Ink: Books with Soul and Spark

These are not stories of young love. They are stories of lives already lived—of hearts that have been tested, broken, guarded, or simply never given the chance to love at all. Written for the silver-haired reader—and for anyone who believes love is more than desire—these novels explore the quiet, powerful longing for connection that doesn't fade with time. Here, love is not lusty or fleeting. It is thoughtful. Earned. Soul-deep. Men and women who have been wounded by love. In each story, something begins. A small shift. A moment of courage. And from that moment, new life grows. These are stories where love overcomes the most dreadful obstacles—where two people learn not just how to love another… but finally accept themselves. And in the end, their love doesn't stop with them. It expands in spiritual ways—touching others, planting seeds of hope, healing, creating possibilities that carry on long after they are gone.

Short Stories-

1.An Older Wine

An Older Wine

Short Stories by Patsy Stanley — Blue WaterCress Ink: Books with Soul and Spark

These are stories that have aged. Not polished to perfection—just lived in. Like an older wine, they carry depth, edge, and the quiet complexity that only time can bring. Across eighteen or so short stories are moments that are funny, bittersweet, unexpected, and sometimes quietly sad. These are glimpses into lives that don't always turn out the way they were meant to… but somehow still hold meaning. You'll meet people who missed their chances. People who found something late. People who didn't know what they had until it was gone. And a few who surprise themselves in the end. There's humor here—sometimes dry, sometimes crooked. There's loss. There's reflection. And now and then… a small grace. These stories don't rush. They linger. Because some truths don't arrive all at once—they deepen over time. *Best read slowly… like something meant to be savored.*

Illustrated Children's books-

1.The Whuzzles
2. The Skaters
The Blue Rubber Albatross
Tom the Owl

Children's Stories Collection

By Patsy Stanley — Blue WaterCress Ink: Books with Soul and Spark

These are stories for little ones—and for the grown-ups who read to them. Filled with gentle adventures, playful characters, and simple, easy-to-follow tales, Patsy Stanley's illustrated children's books are made for young readers just beginning to discover the joy of stories. Each book is lovingly illustrated and written with care—using clear language, soft humor, and just enough imagination to spark wonder without overwhelming young minds. You'll find friendly creatures, small surprises, and comforting moments that invite children to listen, look, and smile.

These are stories meant to be read aloud. Stories to be held, shared, and remembered. Because the first stories a child hears…stay with them forever. *Perfect for toddlers and early readers—and for anyone who believes in gentle beginnings.*

Juvenile Readers

1. Billy Silly Beak and Pearl, the Purple Eared Bird Girl

2. Chef Pepper King and Sir Basil G. Soupstone in The Case of the Disappearing Spy Cat

3. The Dreadful Noises of Landoshar

4. The Rebel Bedats

5. Laundromat Girl

The Ridiculous Tales Collection (For Brave Young Readers)

By Patsy Stanley — Blue WaterCress Ink: Books with Soul and Spark

These are not quiet little stories. They are loud. A little weird. And full of the kinds of things young readers secretly love—body noises, odd creatures, crooked love stories, and characters who don't quite fit anywhere… until they do. Inside this illustrated collection, you'll wander into the world of **The**

Dreadful Noises of Landoshar, where mysterious sounds rumble, pop, and echo—and where learning to laugh at the body's strangest moments becomes part of growing up. You'll meet **Billy Silly Beak**, who falls head-over-feathers in love with Pearl, the purple-eared bird girl—proving that even the most awkward hearts can find their match. And you'll step into the curious kitchen of **Chef Pepper King**, whose unexpected love for Sir Basil Soupstone turns into something far more meaningful than a meal. And , there are more short stories in single file, like Laundromat Girl and The Rebel Bedats. These stories are funny, a little messy, and surprisingly thoughtful—written for readers who are growing, changing, and figuring themselves out. Because somewhere between the weird, the loud, and the ridiculous... there's something real. *For readers ages 10 to 18—and for anyone who still laughs at the wrong things at the right time.*

1. Coming of age- Emerald Hawks Flight- a mountain girls childhood
Emerald Hawks Flight

By Patsy Stanley — Blue WaterCress Ink: Books with Soul and Spark

She was born to the mountains—rooted in land, family, and a way of life that shaped her from the very beginning. But life does not always let us stay where we belong. Uprooted from her home, a young mountain girl is taken north into a world that feels unfamiliar, colder in more ways than one. Surrounded by a different culture, different expectations, and quiet pressures to become someone new, she must learn how to hold on to who she is... while slowly becoming who she is meant to be. This is a story of growing up across years—of family ties that stretch and strain, of belonging and not belonging, and of the quiet strength it takes to endure change. Along the way, something within her begins to awaken. A sensitivity. A knowing. A pull toward something deeper. As she comes of age, she is faced with a choice—to remain where she has been placed, or to step forward into a life of purpose. Her journey leads her into town, where she joins a church and begins the long, uncertain path toward becoming a healer—not just for others, but for herself. *Emerald Hawks Flight* is a story of resilience, identity, and the quiet calling that follows us no matter how far we are taken from home. Because sometimes, to become who we are meant to be…we must first be carried far from where we began.

My Non- fiction- books are-----

The metaphysical series-

1.The Spiritual Nature of Atomic Structure.

2. The Elements

3. Chakras, Meridians, and the Color Energies

4.Shield Energies

5. The Mental body

6. Sound Energies

7.The Four Bodies of Being

8.The Five Outer Chakras and the Etheric Web

9. A Little Book of Rinses